WHITE LILIES

WHITE LILIES

AN ESSAY ON GRIEF

VIDYA KRISHNAN

Published by Tranquebar, an imprint of Westland Books, a division of Nasadiya Technologies Private Limited, in 2025

No. 269/2B, First Floor, 'Irai Arul', Vimalraj Street, Nethaji Nagar, Alapakkam Main Road, Maduravoyal, Chennai 600095

Westland, the Westland logo, Tranquebar and the Tranquebar are the trademarks of Nasadiya Technologies Private Limited, or its affiliates.

ISBN: 9789360451318

10 9 8 7 6 5 4 3 2 1

Typeset by Jojy Philip

Printed at Manipal Technologies Limited, Manipal

For Paati and Ali
Death is Nothing at all

White Lilies

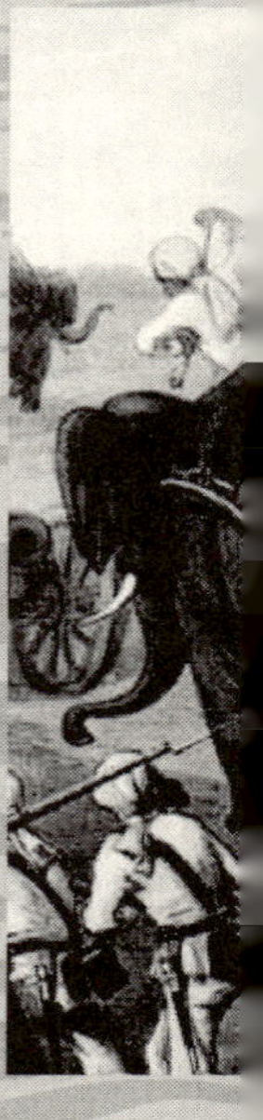

Everyone has things they never get over. Mine is this.

For decades, I have hated Delhi and everyone in it with the vicious pettiness of a lonely mourner. I resent this city, my prison, my home, with the patient bitterness of people who are in relationships that have long been broken, but no one has had the courage to walk away. Its streets, parks and neighbourhoods are both a comfort and a wound. Delhi knows the things I keep locked up.

I was born here, and those born to this city will tell you that we are ill-equipped to cope elsewhere. Other cities seem almost wrongly arranged, spitefully lacking in chaos. Bollywood will have you believe that Delhi welcomes strangers, and history books will remind you that it is no ordinary city. It is, and will always remain, a sanctuary city for misfits on the run. If cities were sexed, then Delhi is definitely female. A gorgeous woman with a pleasing musical speech, lehja. She is prone to melodrama and melancholy, and with age, her face has hardened, she has turned bitter, disputatious and tough as nails. She brags that she belongs to no one, and things that belong to no one implicitly belong to everyone.

The recorded history of Delhi or Dilli, goes back to the eighth century. It is a city that suffered catastrophes, repeatedly rose from the ruins, the many layers of which we drive around today. It is said that the city was built, destroyed and rebuilt at least seven times, giving it a reputation of being the grave of many empires—the Mughal and the British, most recently. The city was ruled by five successful dynasties before them. Unsurprisingly, a rich, fanciful and vast mythology has grown up around Delhi—of its being coveted, destroyed, broken, subdued and reborn, depending on who is telling the story. Delhi is not one of those planned megapolises built to accommodate a people who love the hum of routine. This is a city purpose-built for survival, not for luxury or convenience. It is a sanctuary carved out of humankind's history of invasions and oppression, designed for people who know violence intimately. For people on the run, with no place to call home.

Delhi's reputation as a refugee city goes back to 1258, when Genghis Khan laid siege to Baghdad. As Mongol hordes ravaged kingdom after kingdom, Delhi resisted the invasion and provided refuge to intellectuals, poets and writers fleeing Baghdad. For centuries, wave after wave of armies, poets, craftsmen and migrants have poured into this city, made it their home. They came carrying shards of their brokenness, and also the sparks of something resilient and alive. The poets whose words had been banned, intellectuals who had fled tyrants and the scholars who had been silenced all came to Delhi and found each other, their ideas mingling like spices in the air. Poetry grew in the cracks of this city's pavements, thriving on the alchemy of its dislocated people. Since the thirteenth century, Delhi has remained this way, a press of people and the whiff of amaltas flowers, a city burnt down by invaders over and over again, but simply refusing to die.

It fell to marauders, one after another, in the eighteenth and nineteenth centuries. In 1803, it was captured by the British East India Company (EIC). It became the capital of the newly independent India in 1947 when the British left. In this city, no story has ever been final; even endings as big as those of empires were simply new beginnings.

From all over India, people came to Delhi in search of a better future. Migrants came here looking for a home, and by a process of synthesis and absorption made it what it is. This is where broken things became whole. Ever absorbent, Delhi took in the trauma and the impossible pain of individual tragedies, and found new cuisines, new masters, new residents, and thrived.

There is beauty in it of a kind you can only find in ancient cities like Cairo, Palestine or Athens, where life is lived on the streets. The flower sellers, the bangle makers, locksmiths and chai makers plying their trade, children playing cricket, cars and auto rickshaws and cycles negotiating for space in a megapolis where every inch of the streets is efficiently used.

A city always bursting with life.

There is another version of this story that only those who live here know. It is bursting with death too.

Women are raped in buses; India's ruling class runs it with an iron grip. For half of the year, the air is unbreathable and poisonous, and the roads are among the most dangerous in the world. It is the kind of city urban dystopianists base their stories in. All sorts of accidents can befall people who live here. There is the collective trauma of events like invasions and earthquakes, and the deeply personal tragedies like death by road rage or rape. Here, death is never too far.

In Delhi, we live on a tectonic place, a high seismic zone, next to a six-storey-high mountain of waste at the Ghazipur landfill in the east, knowing that, from time to time, it wakes up groggily and stretches some achy corner, sending down an avalanche of deadly garbage. The last time that happened, people were trapped in their cars as well as on foot. It is an unimaginable way to die in any other city—not Delhi though. Not in this city, where death will never run out of people. Delhi thrives on death the way beasts thrive on blood. The daily grind of survival here can choke the hope out of a person. It is a monster that routinely pulverises the people who make it home.

For decades, it has reminded me of Ouroboros, the serpent eating its own tail; continually devouring itself and being reborn from itself. I am yet to see a city that is in equal measure decaying and regenerating. The Egyptians believe Ouroboros to be completely self-contained, completely self-referential; it feeds, fertilises and engulfs itself, just as Delhi does. Through the ages, the city has retained its fraught duality by being both a utopia as well as a dystopia, a city of palaces and open gutters, a necropolis and a megapolis, where deprivation and greed, begging children and the prime minister, starvation and degustation menus all live cheek by jowl.

To truly understand Delhi, one must understand her relationship with power. This city clings to power like an addict to a final hit—wild, reckless and indifferent to the price it pays. Once I saw a heavily built man in the metro. He was eating tandoori chicken from a large Tupperware box and spitting the bones back in it. The entire coach reeked. The person next to him was clearly uncomfortable. Nobody said a word. Every single person kept looking straight ahead. Later on, a young couple, probably college-going, got into the same coach, their fingers interlocked. They were standing close to each other the way young lovers do. The entire coach stared them down till they released each other's hands, put some distance between their bodies and got off at the next station. That's Delhi.

This explains the central paradox of life in Delhi, one of the grandest and oldest cities of the world, where people behave not with the elegance or sophistication associated with historic, aristocratic cities, but with utmost vulgarity and apathy towards their surroundings. It is perhaps because we expect Delhi to rise from the ruins each time, to survive no matter what we inflict on her that we think we can get away with this abject neglect—apathy towards one another as well as the city. We cannot imagine that Delhi, the grand old city, might also suffer wear and tear, like old cars that give up on a Wednesday morning after a lifetime of being taken for granted. After we've broken it, we will start looking around, hoping we have a spare one somewhere, a functioning city where people are safe in public, instead of this pile of garbage we call home.

Over time, Dilli became 'Old Delhi' as New Delhi expanded around it. No matter how much the town planners tried to create a modern city, it refused to leave behind the graveyard of dynasties. So, we live in a 'New

Delhi' that is not new at all—the crumbling tombs and old mosques stick out in the middle of heavy traffic as roundabouts. Modern homes now nestle beside the soaring grandeur of Mughal architecture. It feels like history had been airdropped into the gaps left by modernity. It is a remarkable feat, teetering between glory and ruin. And all the while, the city swallows up farmlands and villages, with no natural limit to stop it as it grows and grows.

People who live here, like me, tend to talk of the city as if we don't simply live in it; we live *through* it. The traffic, the violence, the chaos, the politics—our lives move to the rhythm of Delhi's mood swings. We navigate a city conjured up by long-dead emperors and their long-dead town planners, one that is simply unfit for the cyclists and pedestrians and car drivers and hawkers and children playing cricket to all go about their lives at the same time. Yet, we do, we choose Delhi every day. We all exist here, quarrel with her when she is mean-spirited and love her when she is generous.

There are many lores about Delhi's tendency to keep returning to life. The more popular one is that djinns loved Delhi too much to see it deserted. It is easy to believe that this was a haunted city. After all, you only have to watch the passing traffic to see people talking to themselves as they go about their busy lives, chasing and being chased by ghosts. Two places in Delhi are believed to be haunted by djinns: the Feroz Shah Kotla fort, built in the fourteenth century, and the Jamali Kamali mosque, one of the lesser-known historic treasures in the Mehrauli Archaeological Park that was constructed in the sixteenth century. It is believed that the fort is haunted by a djinn who demands offerings of fruits and sweets from visitors. Failure to comply is said to result in misfortune. I'm partial to the lore about the Jamali Kamali mosque. People have reported hearing whispers and footsteps and seeing shadowy figures. It is believed that two djinns who reside in the tombs here protect the place from any harm and bless those who visit it with good fortune. The tombs belong to Sheikh Jamal-ud-din Kamboh Dehlawi, a Sufi saint and a poet, and to Kamali, who is either his disciple or lover, depending on who is telling the story.

I don't think we are haunted by djinns. I prefer to believe Delhi is haunted by poets and lovers; people who lived here, in this city, and were pulverised by the burden of it, and decided to haunt the rest of us. The people who died of gang rapes, in traffic accidents or under garbage piles. I would not be surprised to find every house, every street corner haunted by the people who died here of broken hearts.

If Kolkata is the City of Joy, Delhi undoubtedly has to be the City of Grief. Or perhaps of despair. But it is also a place of stellar resilience and beautiful poetry, the kind that takes grief and turns it into the art of losing.

It makes sense to me that Delhi, with its long history of bereavement, was also home to Mirza Asadullah Khan 'Ghalib', who captured grief as perhaps no poet, no one else has. Few who have lived in Delhi are more broken, more ruined and more haunted than Ghalib. People familiar with his work are willing to die on this hill: that if he had written in English, instead of Persian or Urdu, he'd be more popular than Shakespeare. I am one of those people.

His life coincides with the perfect storm of events that was the collapse of the Mughal empire and the takeover of India by the British Crown. He was one of Delhi's more famous lovers. She loved him back, as deeply as only wicked women can. The legend is that, if someone asked him for his address, he'd say, 'Ghalib, Dilli, should be enough.' By the end of his life, the relationship would sour. He would write to a friend that he was 'condemned to live in Delhi as a prisoner' and 'was sentenced to the hard labour of writing prose and poetry'. It is in Delhi's nature to turn on empires, individuals, governments. Poets and journalists are no exception.

Ghalib was part of Delhi's aristo-literary elite, and famous in his lifetime for his quick wit, poetry and letters. He was a notorious bar-crawler, his life an orgy of indulgence. He was arrogant, he gambled and drank like a sailor, and took courtesans to bed. Until the end of his life, he had a deep, abiding love for the good things of life: wine, women, chess and mangoes. Once, someone asked him to reconsider his dissolute lifestyle—he was a prominent Muslim, and openly alcoholic—especially since he had chosen to live right under the shadow of the Grand Mosque, the Jama Masjid.

His response, often quoted by Hindi and Urdu speakers, and in my opinion a good test of his brilliance in turning a phrase, was

> *Masjid ke zer-e-sāya ik ghar banā liyā hai*
> *Ye banda-e-kamīna ham-sāya-e-ḳhudā hai*
> *I have made my house under the protection of the mosque,*
> *A scoundrel must shadow God.*

Emperor Shah Jahan began constructing that mosque in 1650, fifteen years after he commissioned the Taj Mahal. Its courtyard accommodates nearly 25,000 faithful to this day, who stop by the kebab sellers outside after the prayers, just as they have done for centuries. Sufi saints walk around the bazaar, and street performers busk as they have done for centuries.

Ghalib came from a family of aristocratic Turks, and his ancestors occupied important positions in the armies of the Mughals. He was born in Agra in 1797. His father died when Ghalib was five years old. After his father's death, he was adopted by his uncle Nasrullah Beg Khan, who died when he was nine. At thirteen, Ghalib was married to Umrao Begum, who came from a family of similar standing. That's when he moved to Delhi, in 1812—never to find happiness in this city, and never to leave. He was the last of the great Delhi poets, as well as the first of its great modern poets. He straddled two epochs, the Mughal dynasty and British India.

His marriage was unhappy and would last sixty years. It was made unhappier by the fact that he never received the recognition that was his due from the Mughal courts. An aristocrat through and through, Ghalib lived extravagantly, spending borrowed money on expensive wine and even more expensive love affairs. He had seven children, all of whom died in infancy. A nephew he adopted died at eighteen. Eventually, he died a bar-room hero, boozing and swaggering, debt-ridden and heartbroken.

There was so much death in his life that it would become a constant theme in his poetry. Ghalib's grief has an odour that still permeates Delhi. Unlike Emily Dickinson's contained sorrow or Rainer Maria Rilke's visceral poetry, Ghalib's grief was an ocean, terrifying and beautiful. He did not passively mourn loss or treat it as something that had to be exorcised. Ghalib's grief was alive, intimate and sacred. He showed that people do not simply grieve—they *grow* from it. He had the ability to stare at cold bodies, amputated limbs and all the ugly things that came with the British invasion, and turn it into poetry. To this day, from Bollywood heroes to jilted lovers, people continue to use his words to express their sorrows.

The recognition he had craved so long finally came in 1854 when he was promoted to poet laureate in the court of the last Mughal, Emperor Bahadur Shah Zafar. Within three years of this fragile stability, the British would come calling.

When the Mughal empire fell, Ghalib was reduced to a common pensioner who depended on the British for his monthly dole of sixty-two rupees. He would fight a sixteen-year-long legal battle—no less valiant than those fought by his Turkish ancestors—to get his pension increased. After failing, he would write directly to Queen Victoria, sending his petition through the governor general in 1856. He received a promising response in January 1857, four months before the 'Sepoy Mutiny'. That first fight for Indian Independence failed, and left Ghalib devastated. He gritted his teeth and endured the British capture of Delhi and the fall of the Mughal empire.

Ghalib saw his emperor, Zafar—whose name meant victory, ironically—exiled to Burma, his city gutted, his neighbours slaughtered. He carried the dead in his poetry, like bloody souvenirs. His diaries over the next fifteen months would be compiled as *Dastanbuy*, a lament for Delhi and a vivid account of his changing fortunes. It was an upside-down world. The learned became illiterate overnight because they did not speak English. His grief did not recede with the passage of time; if anything, it grew keener, sank deeper roots in his poetry.

Never has a writer been matched to a moment more perfectly.

Ghalib wrote as the British took over the Red Fort, he wrote as his brother died. He wrote as he fell deeper and deeper into debt. He wrote as his children died. He wrote and wrote and wrote. Ghalib wrote as if poetry could accomplish the miracle of stopping the walls from crumbling down.

When lives disintegrate, it is the small things you remember in searing detail. I remember how we used to hold hands walking down streets. We had not had our first big fight yet. We were together all the time when we were not working, and we used to say 'I love you' often. The thing is, you can never know how much you truly love a person. Not until they die.

Ali came into my life abruptly. I was hosting a friend who played tennis with him. When I answered the doorbell that evening, there stood a man with a crooked smile, the kind that began at his mouth and crinkled around the eyes. It was authentic enough to create a feedback loop which made me smile back at this stranger, a thing women in Delhi rarely do. He was a good-looking man, lanky and brown-eyed. That evening, he was wearing blue denim jeans with a white linen shirt, crumpled at the sleeves. He sank into my sofa with the comfort of a man in his own living room, one leg dangling over the other, and held fort.

He had a way of holding people's eyes when he spoke to them. His eyes were warm, radiant, and when they fixed on someone, which was sometimes me, it felt like sleeping under a sunbeam. We were dating before I realised we were. Within five months of our first meeting, he had moved in with me. In those days, my living room was never without white lilies, as he wooed me and tried to convince me to take a spa vacation to Bali *and* meet his family. He was a happy man, in a mad rush to live. He'd later tell me that he knew he was going to marry me as soon as I opened the door. Now, that evening comes back to me in hallucinatory flashes so detailed that it scars me afresh each time.

There are not enough words and not enough ink to describe the chaos of that August. How do you pinpoint the exact moment when your life was destroyed? When exactly did it begin? On the rare occasions that I have narrated this story—

No, that's not right. I have never narrated this story. I have to begin with 23 August 2013. It was a Friday. The marigolds were in full bloom. I left for Bangalore in the morning on a reporting assignment. On Saturday, I cancelled my flight back to Delhi, deciding to drive down to Chennai instead. My grandmother, the only safe space of my childhood, was dying. When I reached her place that night, she was already disoriented. I had not seen her in a year. Her last words to me were a question: have you come in my dream?

I want to believe she heard my answer.

She had started haemorrhaging, and there was nothing for me to do but sit by her, stroke the hand that had become soft and wrinkled with all the effort it must have taken to feed, soothe and love me. I wiped the blood that would ooze from her mouth from time to time. She died surrounded by her sons and several grandchildren. She was loved. I was bereft. I remember standing in front of her just after, stunned . . . like one would be after they were robbed on a highway.

Until this point, I had not known the kind of grief that comes with death. Death I had witnessed amply, as a reporter, on television screens and in over-the-top Bollywood movies. Now, standing by my grandmother's bedside, nothing I had seen compared. We cremated her on Sunday afternoon, and I got on the first flight to Delhi on Monday morning. By the time I reached home, Ali had left for work. We met for a quick lunch that day at a restaurant in the central circle of Connaught Place. I had not seen him for three days. Ali had dinner plans that were made before Paati had died. He offered to cancel and stay home. I would never understand why I insisted he keep his dinner appointment, and bring me soup on the way back.

He never came back.

Someone ran him over. The car behind was speeding too, so he was run over a second time. Someone else stole both his phones. I did not know all night that he had been taken to a hospital. I had spent the night pacing around the house, not knowing whom to call—he could be with his sister or his parents. I did not have their contact details because I had been stubbornly refusing to meet his family. I did catch some sleep that night, and for years, I'd be tormented by the fact that I was asleep while he was dying.

When I finally got the call, it was 6 a.m. the next day. I took down the details: hit by car. Brain stem injury. Vegetative. Trauma centre. ICU. My next call—from the car—was to Dr Sharma, medical superintendent of the trauma centre. Dr Sharma assumed I was calling on behalf of a patient, as I often did. Health reporters in India routinely pull strings to get families medical information from overworked, underpaid and, sometimes, indifferent doctors. Assuming this was one of those calls, the doctor told me that the patient had suffered a stroke during the night. 'His heart is strong, but if he lives, he'll be vegetative. It is likely he will die. Since you know the family, can you please ask them if they'd be open to considering organ donation? You know how things are at the hospital … '

I was on the Ring Road, one of Delhi's arterial roads that connects the southern part to the city's centre, holding on to the steering wheel to keep from reeling. Minutes from the trauma centre he was now at, there was still a pool of blood. Ali's head had hit the divider, his skull had cracked and the brain stem had broken. It caused a pile-up and a traffic jam that made news. There was shattered glass everywhere. In my terminal lucidity, on my deathbed, I'll still be able to see Ali's dried blood that everyone was driving over that Tuesday morning.

I don't remember the rest of the drive to the hospital or parking the car, but I do recall a mad dash to the reception. I was finally meeting his family—inside the trauma centre. His elder sister seemed to know who I was when I got there. 'I'll take you in, but if you are not calm the doctors will make you leave,' was the first thing she said to me. I nodded. Standing by his bed, I remember being stunned by the small pool of his blood on the hospital tile. There was dried blood in the hollow of his ear. In the honeycomb of my brain, every memory from that day is lodged with an unsettling looseness. Things shift and fall out of my brain . . . the heat and the smell of death and disinfectant from the emergency room, the younger patient who was brought in earlier that night, with a serious injury, a patient the doctors believed was likely to survive. And I remember the doctors, despite being short-staffed, despite knowing Ali wouldn't make it, refused to give up on him.

I can remember myself sitting on the floor, looking at his family huddled in a corner, wondering if this was a nightmare.

I'd like to believe that Ali heard what I said to him in there, but pretty much exactly like my grandmother, Ali started haemorrhaging too. When I came back out, his sister asked me if we had discussed organ donation. 'No. We were discussing spa vacations,' the words fell inertly from my mouth.

It took him another day to die.

After two days, Ali, whom I had loved intensely, lay intensely dead on a gurney. Our story had ended as abruptly as it had begun. I had such little to show for it. Two photos, to be precise. Everything else was on his phone. Which had been stolen, like the life I would have had. The last I saw him was over a pasta lunch, during which he had joked about being better-looking than me. And here he was, his perfectly proportionate face that broke into a generous smile every time I saw him swollen beyond recognition, smelling of the congealed blood that was matted in his hair. This too I remember, the smell of blood eternally fresh on the tongue. Brooding over his body were me and his family—strangers sharing a sacred, quiet space. The kind of quiet that follows defeat. His defeat to life, and ours to death.

The thing about death is that the loss you feel the day a person dies is simply an inciting event. If you live long enough, you lose them repeatedly as long as you live and they do not. The grief pounds in you like a headache, making it impossible to see and breathe and smile and eat. By the end of the first week, I could not tell what I felt. If 'impossible' could be a feeling then that's what I felt most. What are the odds that you lose the two most important people in your life in the span of a weekend? Somehow that is exactly what had happened.

Other emotions would return later, like sea trash expelled by the high tide. I felt guilt for not visiting Paati often enough. For invading a deeply private moment for Ali's family, who, thankfully, had the largeness of heart to take me in. For somehow not dying from the pain it caused, like a cockroach that survives a nuclear winter. I felt exhausted, mostly, for the first month. I felt exhausted, but not the sort of exhausted you are at the end of a long day. The kind of exhausted you are when you've been to more funerals than you are supposed to at a certain age. I spent the first week too exhausted to sleep, emotionless, bad-tempered, heavy-lidded, walking around spoiling for a fight. I had not slept since that weekend I left for the reporting assignment in Bangalore. It was also the first time I understood the meaning of true cruelty. Nothing matches the cruel finality of death, of the suddenly silent body.

The next time I saw him, he was on a stretcher wrapped in white cloth, with a sticker on his head that identified him. Rigor mortis had set in. I put my hand on his still body and felt panic rise at the idea of him—his hands, his warm eyes, his skin—being suffocated in that shroud. I remember saying the word 'shroud' to myself to help it make sense. For the second time that week I was at a funeral.

We lowered him into a grave on Thursday evening. The day itself was cruel. Overcast skies and a mournful August air that could rip your heart out of your chest, followed by a downpour that I would normally have enjoyed. The sky had been swirling with dark clouds all week. On the day of his funeral, it felt as if all the tension had condensed in the sky above, transformed on this unalterable, horrible day into raw physical force. We embalmed him and buried him under soft brown mud. I remember his three-year-old niece being surprised to learn that grown-ups cry too. No one ever warns you about days like these: when hell resides in the pit of your stomach, when you must breathe through a bottomless black hole. I drove back to our apartment, put his laundry in its place and shut the door on Delhi, this wretched, brute of a city. For hours that night I stared at the ceiling.

There had been so many people at the funeral that I didn't know. I went through the rituals of mourning, thinking, certain of it, that once everything was over and everyone was gone, I'd get to sit down for a conversation with Ali. It is scary the kind of tricks your mind can play on you. I had genuinely convinced myself that, when no one else was around, I'd get a final conversation to resolve what was left unsaid.

After all the obvious tasks of mourning were completed—the funeral service was over, the death certificate obtained, his clothes handed back to his siblings, the visitors had gone—I had no idea what else to do. I had lost all interest in the outside world as well as the long-term implications of my plight (if that's what it was—a plight) under the pressure of having to live hour after hour.

In the weeks after, I'd go every day to his muddy grave, thinking about how I was mad at him for not coming home or calling me to say he was going to be late. All night, I was mad at him when I should have been with him. Did he know how sorry I was? I think not. I'd sit by his grave, clicking photos of how the sun fell on the white lilies that I had placed where his chest was, six feet under.

I'd keep track of newer graves that had been dug since my last visit. There was lots to do for me here. His grave was peaceful, with grass waving above him, a spot of silence in the middle of a roaring city. For years, I'd want to dig my way in, out of envy for his eternal peace. And my profound bereavements.

Death had made me face some simple yet confounding facts: that all of us are hurtling towards an end, yet none of us are facing it. That the ground we walk on and the castles we build on them are fickle. But forced to face death, my brain was rebelling. The whole week had been weirdly normal, and yet not normal at all. The inexplicable and the mundane had joined hands, and nothing made sense. It was, in fact, the ordinary nature of everything that came after the two funerals that prevented me from truly believing this had happened, or absorbing it in any real way. It was only after my grandmother's death that I realised how much of her was in me, in my cooking, in my fanatic clean-as-you-go principle that spilled over from the kitchen to every aspect of my life. When she died, I realised I had lost a part of my own identity. No one would ever tell me again that 'a good cook is one who can make a feast and leave the kitchen looking like it has not been used at all'.

Then there was the loss of Ali to deal with. It was bizarre that he was . . . dead. His lawyer's robe and shaving kit and laptop . . . and me . . . everything was waiting for him. Everything was suspended in the emptiness. The violence of it had smashed all the 'rules' I knew—what to say, how to behave, when to cry, when to speak, when to eat. Reality had dissolved and been replaced by the incomprehensible. I'd seen this pattern over and over as a journalist, and yet, I was in no way prepared for it. In 2005, as a city reporter, I had interviewed many people who were shopping in Sarojini Nagar market when a bomb went off near a juice shop. Without exception, these people began their accounts by telling me what an 'ordinary Thursday' it had been until the explosion. When the lockdown was announced, and the plague inched closer, people would say the same, how they were going about their ordinary day that March when the pandemic struck. It was the ordinariness of Ali's death that would haunt me the most.

Most people are loath to linger in loss. We are expected to get back to work, back to normal, mostly to make people around us feel better. Not me. I made it my full-time job. I simply sat and stared at my wound for years. This burden of my own grief was so heavy that I simply couldn't shake it off after a night on the town or a good pep talk. I found myself weighed down by what had come to pass and carried it around like a snail carries its house on its back.

Writing about other people's grief is easy. Your own grief, that is black ink on black pages. I could say what it felt like—someone had poured my heart into a blender and made me drink it back again. That my heart was still in my rib cage and beating, but it was . . . scrambled. That still wouldn't capture the half of it. Damn August to hell. The month of marigolds, monsoon and mayhem.

Other people heard the news and were shocked, although with that secret note you can sense in the tone of people receiving bad news that, whatever it was, it had not happened to them. It was some feeble stew of sympathy, compassion, political correctness and general indifference, and it made me vomit. No one really cared about the deaths. They were simply grateful for *their* life. Death makes people—those not touched by it—move away from those in its grip, as if dying is not the result of accidents and infections, but its own disease. If you come too close, you may catch the contagion.

That entire year, I kept losing things, small and big. I'd lose my car keys and wallet with my driving licence in it. I lost my ability to read. I'd lose patience during edit meets, suddenly be reduced to tears in the middle of a perfectly normal conversation. I lost my appetite and my sanity. I lost many friends who did not know how to be around someone in such palpable pain. Perhaps the best thing that can be said about loss is that, after a point, when you have nothing left to lose, it can liberate you. The defining emotion of losing things big and small was, for me, not panic, but a search for meaning.

The loss of small things—the keys and jackets and books and scarves—evoked the same reaction in me as my big losses: where are they now? What happened after me? If I only knew what happened to my wallet—that I left it in a cafe and someone who needed the money took it and tossed the rest of it in the garbage—I'd have closure. In search of meaning, I was putting my small losses to the same level of scrutiny as my big ones, but it is one thing to lose a wallet and completely another to lose your partner. All I wanted for years was closure. Something, anything at all that could help me make sense of that bloody weekend—nirvana, wormholes, afterlife.

I grilled my few trusted friends on the idea of the afterlife. I found nothing, either in Hinduism or Islam, so I went to speak to a forensic pathologist at the hospital where Ali had died. I learnt that, within seventy-two hours of death, our internal organs start decomposing, and between eight to ten days, our body starts to liquify. The thought of Ali, who had just returned from Everest Base

Camp and was training for the Delhi marathon, liquifying in his grave was so bizarre to me. Since I lost—a curious word to attach to death—Ali and Paati, I, too, was lost, adrift, rudderless and in a shambles. This kind of grief is not a transitional state, but a terminal one.

I filed the story that had sent me to Bangalore that week. I filed another story, about increasing road accidents in Delhi, packed it with data and quotes from activists to show how dangerous Delhi's roads were. Even though we were a financial newspaper, I think my editor let me write it because I was in no state to handle a story being turned down that week. What I wanted to write was . . . all of this. I have heard that we write about things we cannot process by other means. I wanted to vomit out my grief on a piece of paper, remove it from my body like you do with malignant tumours. It would take me ten years to put pen to paper. Instead, I wrote about the dangers of Delhi's roads, feeling more organically and personally bound to this city I hated because someone I loved was buried here.

Ali's family held a beautiful memorial service. His sister read out *Death Is Nothing at All* by Henry Scott-Holland. His uncle read out *Farz Karo* by Ibn-e-Insha. I left white lilies in front of a photo I had clicked during one of our last lunches together; it had been blown up and garlanded. I had a feeling Ali would find it funny. He was looking at me with deadpan eyes, irritated that I had pulled out the phone in the middle of a conversation. It was the kind of photo where you felt its eyes follow you around the room. How could he, or I, have known that this would be the photo in the obituary and memorial service and my dining room? A futile attempt to capture the essence of him.

Everyone who loved him realised they only knew fragments of him. Gathered at his memorial, we were trying to piece him back together with new anecdotes about the time he had lent money to someone quietly, or got someone else a job without bragging about it, or how he had cried watching *Kabhi Khushi Kabhie Gham*, and his siblings rolled their eyes when I said he had cried during *Bhaag Milkha Bhaag* too. He cried easily and felt deeply. His cousins and friends shared stories about him, shared a video of him laughing, surrounded by family. The video was set to the Beatles's *In My Life*. It almost made dying sound meaningful—and it is true that, if you are lucky, people you loved will come together and celebrate you after your death. We learnt new things about him at his wake. Perhaps there is meaning to be found within it, some sort of a silver lining to a dark cloud that will follow me for the rest of my life. Still, a dark cloud is a dark cloud.

That Scott-Holland poem claims death 'does not count'. It is like 'slipping into the next room'. He wrote:

Everything remains exactly as it was.
I am I, and you are you,
and the old life that we lived so fondly together is
untouched, unchanged.
Whatever we were to each other, that we are still.

The death we encounter in poetry is so beautiful, so different from the ugly version we live with. If Ali and Paati were in the 'next room', could they not hear me wail? I wanted to cross-examine his sister, but I also never wanted to speak again. There was nothing to say and no one to say it to. They were gone and I had to carry on.

They asked me if I wanted to speak at the memorial. My first reaction was to check with Ali about this. Then I remembered he had died. There had been an accident. I had to repeat it to myself the entire week, starting from my Paati's death to the current moment to keep hold of sanity. I did not speak at his memorial. I had nothing to say unless what I said could rewind time itself. I did manage to maintain my composure during the service. Ali had been reading Jon Krakauer's *Into the Wild* the night before. For the next four years, it would remain at the bedside, just as he left it.

My boyfriend was dead. My grandmother was dead. And I couldn't shake the sense that another shoe was about to drop, that at any moment I would learn that someone else close to me had died. If someone did not answer my phone, I assumed they had died. Someone had stolen their phone too. I'd use that to fall into another tidal wave of anticipatory grief. That is exactly what happened.

Three weeks after these deaths, on 21 September 2013, four masked gunmen attacked the Westgate shopping mall, an upmarket mall in Nairobi, Kenya. The militant group al-Shabaab claimed responsibility for the incident in which seventy-one people died. Two of them were my cousins. My brother-in-law was killed immediately, and my cousin underwent facial reconstruction surgery after the bullet entered her jaw and exited from the other side. This loss was not the same as the ones I was grieving, but it solidified a feeling in the pit of my stomach that the sky was falling and there was no escape. By now I had said so many goodbyes—to people I loved, to the life I used to have, to normal things like friends and brunch. I had yielded to the grief and found that it was not enough. Imagine being prepared to do that, to have nothing more to yield, to be broken, yet to be pressed to yield more. That's where I was. No matter how much pain I was in, the sun rose again and again. By the time I got to December of that year, the grief I felt wasn't just an emotion. It had altered my eating and sleeping patterns, it was a physical presence in my body, as real as the teeth in my mouth.

By the end of the year, Delhi's famous winter had set in. With it, came an additional sense of gloom and a thick blanket of smog. It is the kind of gloom you find in dystopian cities that have erased the concept of a blue sky. The wind, blowing in steadily from the north, was bringing with it poisoned air. The sky was full of fine dust that would eventually settle in our lungs. It was a different kind of siege Delhi was under. Smog rather than air was the medium in which we lived; we swam in the metallic-tasting dust. On the worst days, schools were suspended. It became acceptable for people who could afford to be gone for a few months to wait out the apocalyptic air. The rest of us, with kids in schools and jobs and graves to tend to, were still here. Where was I going to go anyway?

Regardless of the inner turmoil, I still had to wake up every morning, eat, shower and head to work, and do my laundry and pay my bills. When I met people, they patted me on the back for 'being brave' and 'getting through it'. They had no way of knowing how far from the truth that was. When people asked me how I was, the only thing I could do was lie. Out of politeness. Out of exhaustion. How do you answer that question, without, piece by piece, explaining what is happening inside you? When you cannot even explain that to yourself? Besides, everything people said to me, I had heard before—how sorry they were, how worried they were about me, how unfair it all was. This period taught me to deeply love people who could sit quietly in the discomfort of someone else's grief. People like me, who were also too tired to speak, and did not need to fill the absence with insincere words. They spoke silence fluently.

I got a lot of inappropriate 'help' in those days. One friend gifted me a book about a girl who'd lost her boyfriend tragically, only to find out that he was now haunting her. Another friend encouraged me to watch the episode from *Black Mirror* about a young woman whose boyfriend is killed in a car accident. She brings him back to life using a software mimicking dead people. Despite being surrounded by death, we seem to not know when a mourner will welcome expressions of sympathy or prefer the pretence that nothing has really happened. Both made me angry. A few months after that weekend, a friend tried to convince me that it was time to 'let it go', as my grief was making people around me, herself included, uncomfortable. I never spoke to her again. If my journalism career tanks, I intend to start a grief consultancy, advising idiotic friends on how to be there for grieving people.

The two people I lost were making me re-balance every other relationship I still had.

When I woke up the morning after Ali had been buried and my grandmother cremated and a memorial service attended—all of it was single long day to me—I was certain I would find Ali on his side of the bed, complaining about how cold he was all night. He died again in the morning when I woke up and no one was complaining about the air conditioner. For several months, that's how I would wake up, bewildered, like a person with and without short-term memory loss. Both of them died many times in those days. When I wanted my grandmother's recipe for lemon rasam and realised I couldn't just call her. When the white lilies turned an ugly colour of death, but they were in a living room that Ali was not in, so no one would toss them out and replace them with a fresh batch. I'd forget briefly or sleep, only to wake up dizzy, confused, thirsty. I could never recall if I had eaten, or who had restocked the fridge with eggs and milk and bread. It felt as if a tank had rolled over me, twice, and even though my phone told me it was eight in the morning, I was so far from light that it felt like the darkest and longest day.

Sometimes I'd think about the man who ran over Ali. Did he feel guilt? Did he feel responsible? Was he drunk?

Texting perhaps? Did he drive better now? Did he still feel in control behind the wheel?

We had so many plans, like all new lovers. Marriage. A small apartment with big windows. A bigger car for the weekend getaways. Friends popping by. Music always playing in the background.

In one of my interminable internal monologues, I told myself that it was, statistically, a matter of time for someone I loved to die on these streets. Everyone has a story about the ugliness we encounter on the streets, behind wheels. I have covered such stories, and I have driven past such accidents. Everyone in Delhi knows someone who died in a road accident. Like people in Paris are likely to know a baker and people in London are likely to know stock market analysts.

The story I carry in my bones is repeated over and over in this city. We are, after all, recklessly driving a tank on crowded streets, without seat belts and traffic laws. The government, while doing nothing at all about it, records approximately 3,00,000 deaths in road accidents annually. For context, that is around 50,000 more deaths than from tuberculosis, the deadliest infectious disease. Any other country would want to do something about it—not India, where we will never run out of people.

If you've lived in Delhi, you have for certain witnessed the macabre sight of a road accident: a shredded tyre, a mangled frame of steel, a bloody shoe, shattered glass. And if you truly belong to Delhi, you've simply driven past it without registering the violence because it has not happened to you. Not today, at least.

In the forty years that I have known Delhi, its population has doubled. The number of cars, however, has quadrupled. The city has more cars than Mumbai, Kolkata and Chennai combined. This is likely because Delhi also has wider roads on which we can all be crammed together. All of us with bad tempers, abusive bosses, bad marriages and cheating partners take out our anger in the only place where no laws apply and we have absolute power: the mean roads of Delhi. There is so much death on Delhi's streets that everyone—courts, police, media, the rest of us—is unfazed when we run into it there. We drive past it, moan about the traffic, in some cases steal from the dying person, but never pause, truly slow down enough to change or even to think of a different way to be. This is us. And our eyes have adjusted to how ugly that is.

My grief had broken down the act of driving into the several trivial, careless acts of brutality we commit behind the wheels. The casual violence of honking at a pedestrian or overtaking a smaller vehicle or speeding in a residential neighbourhood, all of it made me retch. I was suddenly faced with the reality of how ordinary my grief was; how ordinary it was to die on the roads of Delhi. It had been going on for a good while, without me, in something of a parallel world, where people died on the streets or a bus ran over a family. It meant nothing to me because it wasn't someone I knew.

I used to be a careless, foul-mouthed driver who thought of pedestrians as a nuisance as I rushed to a job where, frankly, if I reached ten minutes late or even an hour late, no one would care. But I had to rush, rush, rush . . . In Delhi, we are all in a hurry. Quick meals, on-the-go coffee, fleeting conversations. The speed in and of itself is the destination as we hurtle towards dead-end jobs and dead-end lives. We don't slow down because, if we did, it would give us time to think about how we behave. How what we do affects people around us. That, for certain, would haunt us for the rest of our lives.

Grief makes you slow down, look at horrifying moments in slow motion. Perhaps for that reason, life as well as driving can get scary if you slow down long enough to *really* look at the people on the roads: the children begging at traffic signals, the constable inhaling poisonous fumes day in and day out. If you saw them as flesh and bone, if you started noticing the rich inner lives of people you've trained yourself to unsee, you might have to change. It might make you worry about pedestrians and cyclists. If you could really slow down and feel the weight of it all—bad driving, ghoulish behaviour, hurled abuses—you might collapse under ugliness of it all. It is easier to be blind.

After Ali died, it was difficult for me to unsee how driving works in India, which has one of the most brutal and hierarchical ways of organising traffic known to human society. To outsiders, the traffic may seem chaotic, but that's the reductive view of someone who has not stewed for a lifetime in Delhi's traffic. Those of us who've known only this know how far from chaos it really is. We know that Delhi's traffic is, in fact, governed rigidly by the pettiness of power and is an intricate dance of dominance with hierarchy etched into every engine's roar and every break's squeak. That unmissable element of class warfare is entirely representative of our lives lived off the road; no rules apply to the powerful, and the powerless aspire to breaking rules so they can get a small taste of power.

On these unlawful roads, as in our brutally organised societies, might is right. A bus can weave through the streets like a dupatta on a breezy evening, and a Mercedes will simply have to defer to it. The Mercedes can do the same to a smaller car, which will do the same to an autorickshaw that will pass on the meanness to a cyclist in an unending pay-it-forward nightmare of callous brutality. A driver wrapped in a casket of comfort and safety, cooled by an air conditioner set perfectly to their liking, will not think twice before oppressing a rickshaw puller using his body weight to move every inch. We drive with the self-awareness of a concrete block. Many of us do it without using seat belts, helmets or side-view mirrors, oftentimes drunk behind the wheel, proud of jumping signals. And we do so on roads without kerbs, lane markings, speed limits or working traffic signals. If it is the rainy season, there is the additional, casual cruelty of drenching pedestrians with mucky rainwater spray. The only time something feels like injustice is when it happens to us. Then we broadcast our rage by leaning hard on the horn as if that could give us immediate catharsis. But there is no catharsis to be had.

Years after Ali died, I was reading Dr B.R. Ambedkar's 'Castes in India', a paper he wrote for a Columbia University seminar in 1916, where he defined caste as an 'ascending scale of reverence and a descending scale of contempt'. The words jumped off the page for me, since etched in my brain as the best explanation of driving etiquette in India. People who like new ideas, talk of emancipating the poor, and have Arundhati Roy and James Baldwin on their bookshelves, get behind the wheels and turn into faceless, nameless, combustible monsters. They are not too different from the trolls on social media who hate and bully for no reason at all.

Our roads are poisoned through and through, with most of us driving in a state of habitual revenge. We are our ugliest on the roads, which in itself would have been a crisis worth screaming about from the rooftops in any other city. Not Delhi though. Here, driving is an act of daredevilry taken to *Clockwork Orange* levels. I know people who find it funny when they scare pedestrians or bully small cars into corners. In these fleeting moments, India's vast middle class can rule the roads, finding perverse glee in the humbling of someone lower still. A joy born not from strength but impotence—a perfect example of Delhi's otherwise powerless middle class' overweening ambition to dominate someone, anyone.

All of us, the kind, the cruel, the rich and the poor, drive in a manner that could kill any of us.

The one thing we are not while driving is accommodating, not of the malnourished rickshaw puller using his body weight in blistering heat to get by, or the mother with kids and groceries, or the elderly couple struggling to navigate a busy road. We are a feral people. I could accuse drivers of many things, and all of them would be true. What I truly detest though is our brain-searing hypocrisy. The duplicity of how much we complain about other people's driving.

At the bottom of the hierarchy on the streets of Delhi is the person with the least entitlements and plenty of duties: the pedestrian. They have to be on their best behaviour at all times. From the DTC bus to the cyclists, everyone responds to pedestrians with irritation at best and ferocity at worst. Any act of insubordination—like trying to claim space on a busy road—can result in disproportionate punishment, like punches being thrown, and occasionally death. And that's what Ali was that night: a pedestrian. He had asked his driver to bring the car around because it was easier to cross the road than to take a U-turn at South Extension during rush hour.

Like other marginalised groups in India, this one too has been betrayed by virtually every level of government. The policing of traffic is limited to shaking down drivers or slowing them down with barricades or halting them entirely to serve VIP traffic. It is not geared to serving the public or making the roads safer. Traffic rules in India are shaped by a soil that is simply incompatible with the idea of sharing power or behaving respectfully with someone you share public space with. On these streets, the vehicle and the driver are a single, fused organism—each deriving power from the other. The bigger the vehicle, the worse the driver. If India were to introduce a Finland-like policy of income-based fines for traffic violations, not a single rich driver would pay. It is not for nothing that Delhi's favourite war cry on the streets is, *Tu jaanta hai mera baap kaun hai?* The overuse of this phrase highlights both a desire for dominance and a fundamental insecurity, emblematic of the middle class' struggle for recognition and power.

My mind reeling with road rage and death, I fought panic every time I was in a car. I didn't want to start a crusade or become a road safety activist. I simply wanted to get by without hurting someone with my car. When a pedestrian came too close, my heart raced. When I saw parents walking with their children on the dangerous side of the road, I'd pull over and tell them not to do that. I was a mad woman accosting people around the city, telling them how to walk on these deadly streets. Driving in Delhi left me feeling under siege. Nearly every time I drove, I thought I'd drive over someone. I didn't mind dying in a road accident but was terrorised by the idea that I could hurt someone's son, daughter or partner by my carelessness.

A well-meaning friend, who routinely texted while driving and fervently believed he did not need to wear seat belts, found my views on driving to be good 'engagement bait'. We tossed between us the kind of lopsided back and forth in which one party has no genuine interest in the subject under discussion, while the other is traumatised by the content of it. One day, he was eating a sandwich while driving, with the other hand switching from the gear to the steering, prompting me to comment on how unsafe that was.

'This is how everyone drives,' he said. 'You can't expect everyone to change because something triggers you.'

'It's not about my experience. It's about how you could hurt someone else,' I told him.

'So, what's the solution? I drive like an automaton? In a city where everyone else drives like a maniac? You should, perhaps, not sit in the front seat if it terrifies you.'

I shook my head. What was the use of arguing?

If the traffic violations cost him heavily, he would sing a different tune, I was sure. It didn't even have to be money, perhaps it should not even be money. If violations were met with community service sentencing—clean up landfills or sweep the neighbourhood garbage dump—more thought would go into how we drove. It is a good bet that time is more valuable than money for all the drivers that speed past each other in a race to the bottom. It would also shatter the gender and caste barrier—imagine rich,

Indian men doing the radical act of cleaning up after themselves.

'There's no solution,' I said instead, trying to wind up this pointless exchange. Have you felt it too? That your closest friends love you, but the things that are the most important to you mean nothing to them? It's not even a blip on their existence.

'No solution? Then why have this conversation?'

'Fair enough. I meant there isn't a single solution to solve our traffic problems. Instead there are millions of solutions. You could be one of them if you choose it.'

None of my big-car-driving, latte-swilling, busy friends had any interest in this conversation. They simply wanted things to change without having to play a part in that process. They were all happy to follow local etiquette while driving rented cars in San Francisco or London. Just not in Delhi. I quietly stopped meeting people.

I'd drive and flashes of Ali's blood on the road would assault me. Or I'd imagine someone suddenly stepping onto the road. I'd have detailed images of glass cutting through the person I'd hit, and wonder if he had a girlfriend waiting for soup at home. I'd choose smaller lanes over main roads, assuming they would be slower roads, and adding another layer of assumption that they would be safer. There are no safe roads in Delhi. This is not a city where people understand that the driving licence is a social contract to keep each other safe. There is a rage and casual violence in everyday life that we accept, and if we return home safe on any given day, we are simply lucky. The thing with luck is that it runs out. That day in August, my luck just ran out.

The few friends I had remaining were either firefighters or builders. Those who came to the hospital helped with the logistics of dying. And then there are friends who came later, after the deaths, to quietly stock the kitchen with supplies, clean the house, make it so it doesn't reek of death. I was thankful for them, but the only company I wanted was of my grief, which now felt like a comfortable well-worn tee shirt. I learnt to develop my own relationship with grief, my own myths about it. I suffered and struggled with it until an answer came to me from the depth of this nothingness. I did not believe the answer that emerged bestowed meaning on what had come to pass. Rather, I had simply found a story I needed to tell myself on the off-chance that it could help me feel better.

We rarely talk of how much anger is folded into grief. The sting of a laughter in full peal could send me into a rage, my fists and jaws would clench. The happiness of other people would bear down on me every day. I couldn't remember what it ever felt like to laugh in public. It felt naked. Ugly. The more I heard it, the angrier I got with myself for wanting and not wanting it. The self-centredness of happy people—without the decency to tone it down a notch out of courtesy to those grieving—made me hate everything and everyone in Delhi.

I had this overriding sense of anxiety about how no one else seemed to be struggling with death. Wasn't death the only thing we had in common? How come no one was talking about it? How did everyone else know what to do? Why did they not share? It drove me crazy, drove me to be viciously petty because I was somehow mourning alone in a city bursting with death.

My friends, not knowing what else to say, asked to see a therapist in the hope that it would make me feel better. I didn't want to feel better. I wanted the weekend rewound. Undone. Anything else on offer would just send me into a blinding rage. When I received invitations to the weddings of other people, I wanted them to die. I wanted terrible things to happen to people who advised me to 'move on'. Hearing that from people whose happiness had not been sabotaged by Delhi was like hearing someone with a full belly telling you that your hunger will pass.

I wanted their parents to die and fortunes to be lost, and for them to develop tuberculosis and go deaf. I wanted their armour of happiness smashed to smithereens on a busy street in Delhi, and for everyone to drive over it. When I saw a man with a fracture on the road, or someone with their grandparents, I wanted them to die too. Or die instead. Anything, anyone to die, but my paati and my Ali. Instead of looking for closure, I kept pretending their deaths—inextricably tied—were a negotiation. Until I was left facing the finality of it.

That's not fair, I remember thinking. Because, I mean, what's a person supposed to do with *that*?

There was no closure to be had for me. It sounded like a distant construct, a punchline to a joke I would never understand. I do see why 'closure' is a popular idea at a time when all of us are walking around with festering wounds, in search of salve. We tell ourselves that, if we worked hard, with closure as a goal, maybe we would get there. So we grieve in stages and rely on literature as if this were a matter of finding the right doctor, the right diagnosis and the right medicine. That wasn't for me. I did not want to 'solve' my grief. I wanted to mourn quietly, persistently, as if it were my life's purpose. I wanted to merge with the grief, which was the last remaining connection I had to the people I had lost.

For my grandmother, I felt regret for the time I had let pass, for things unsaid, for my inability to share in any real way who I had become. She was the first person I had wanted to impress. Out of seemingly nothing, she could cook a meal that could provoke food fights if the portions were not equally distributed among her several grandchildren. None of the recipes she taught me had specific measurements. It was always a pinch of this and a dash of that—intuitive cooking that focused on smell and taste, on being present with what I was creating. It was cooking as an act of mindfulness. From meal prep to making the actual dish, the experience of cooking can be almost meditative. She'd turn around and clean up her station, put away food scraps and wash dishes with an efficiency of movement that you might perhaps find in Michelin-star restaurants. When she was done, the counter space would be uncluttered and the sink empty. Not once do I recall her rushing in the kitchen. It was relaxing to watch her, silent and rhythmic, but also precise as a German sniper.

I do not remember a single bad meal from her kitchen. I learnt all the core concepts of cooking—mise en place, clean-as-you-go, zero waste—from my years watching her cook. Perhaps it took her longer, perhaps she'd have a different version of this story, but to my mind, she could conjure up a full spread—poriyal, rasam, curd rice and appalam—before any of us were throwing hunger tantrums. The food was simple and perfect. Then came my favourite part: she would bring everything she had prepared and place it on the floor, next to her. She'd have us all sit facing her and serve us one at a time. Rice first. Then ghee. Then the poriyal. She'd keep a close eye on who's eating how much in a way only grandmothers do. She remembered what each one of us liked the most and cooked that often, and with love.

My favourite thing she made was rasam. In a light broth of tamarind water, she liked to crush tomatoes and green chillies with her hands. Once it came to a boil she added crushed pepper and cumin seeds that were waiting in her mortar and pestle. She'd let it simmer for a few minutes before she popped some mustard seeds in hot ghee, doused the tamarind broth in it and topped it with coriander, and the simplest of dishes was ready to be had—vibrant, fresh, alive. She taught me how to treat herbs with respect. I loved her lemon rasam the most. It is a dish I go to when I am sick, when I am sad or when I want to show off. Now I had lost the recipe and the recipe-keeper, and I'd spend a decade trying to recreate it. Every time I made it, I wondered what was missing. I wondered how she made it. Did she have some trick that I never thought to ask?

I have subsequently learnt, from the academic literature on grief, that this 'searching behaviour', the impulse to make meaning out of meaninglessness, is common among the bereaved. Now that she had passed, I felt I had lost the glorious minutiae of watching her in action, her idiosyncrasies. She was my last connection to my large, extended family. Her death fundamentally changed who we were to each other, meeting each other less and less frequently until we became complete strangers.

I cast my mind back to the black-and-white photos in which she still has dark hair, trying to reach an image of her as she was before me. I want to see her as she was once, young. Younger than that, a little girl in a village in Tanjore. Did she have pigtails? I wish I had asked her these questions. Strain as I do, my first image of her is as my grandmother. In a nine-yard sari, cooking something with me dangling on her shoulder. Those years immediately after her death were filled with guilt that I was not grieving her as much as I was grieving Ali. It was my personal misery Olympics, and Paati was losing. And it wasn't just me; often people either say nothing when I talk about Paati's death or they change the subject back to Ali without acknowledging her loss. It was understandable, I suppose. She was in her eighties and had lived a full life filled with children and grandchildren, and so it didn't count as much. For them.

With Ali, I felt the loss of my future. I had lost my past and my future in one weekend. To make sense of my own impossible pain, to dwell on it and sit with it, was an act of indulgence. And I indulged myself. I cried myself to sleep. I cried in the car. I cried in the bathroom stalls in my newsroom. I cried till I forgot how my face looked when my eyes were not swollen. I cried everywhere, hiding paroxysms of grief behind oversized sunglasses. No matter how much I cried, that Ali-shaped hole in my heart remained.

It dislodged me so firmly and deeply that I had no sense of who I was—like a ship that had lost its keel. There was so much white noise in my head, and I tried everything to quieten it. Running, meditation, yoga. Drowning myself in work. Being absent from work for long periods.

Now I see that my insistence on hanging on to my routine—a job and a long drive to work and filing a pointless story—was a survival instinct. I didn't care about anything or anyone but I kept turning up for work because it kept me busy and made me tired, and I could have a dreamless night if I truly exhausted myself. The rituals and the repetition were fragile threads I held on to so I could weather that storm.

I had already delivered the definitive news to my friends. My newspaper knew about it. The city of Delhi knew about it because his family had published an obituary in the *Times of India*. Yet, I was not sure if any of it was true. I wanted the world to stop spinning, just for a bit. At some deep level, I believed this was a reversible mistake, and if I were alone for long enough and did the maths right, I'd figure out how to fix this, he'd come back with my soup and we could just . . . live a little. If I could not conjure such magic then I wanted some other kind of enchantment, something that could make me forget everything that had happened.

I had read that you end up losing track of time when grief-struck, and it hadn't meant anything to me before my losses. I didn't understand how days can be both long and short at the same time. The days were long to live through, but they were so monotonous that they bled into each other. They didn't have names anymore, just yesterday and tomorrow. One day I realised it had been nine months since Paati and Ali had died. I believed it, but I didn't understand how that could be true. For me, it was one long, unending weekend, still unfolding.

On most nights, I dreamt of them. In one dream, I am trudging across a horrible gridlock on some street. It has to be Delhi. I suddenly run into Ali. He is alive! But he doesn't see me. Or want to talk to me anymore. Every time I approach him, he melts into the air. I later learn that it's because he saw how difficult it has been for me to move on and doesn't want to dismantle my fragile stability. So, I had to move on because he died, and now he won't return because I moved on. I have different versions of this dream and wake up from them half mad.

The most important thing that became wholly unavailable to me after Ali died was life as it would have been had he put a ring on my finger. The life we would have built together. It is in this period that I returned to Ghalib's poetry.

On a hot day in May 2024, I decided to go on a 'Ghalib walk', led by a historian who would take me through the streets the poet roamed, telling 'tales of love, poetry, and the indomitable spirit of Delhi'. While other cities showcase their histories and monuments, in Delhi we live around them, knowing the city will soon obliterate whatever has managed to survive so far. There are no plaques or boulevards guiding you to Ghalib's residence. In guidebooks for tourists, Old Delhi is the kind of place that gets referred to as a 'maze of streets' or a 'tangled web' with 'small lanes'. The city's founder, Emperor Shah Jahan, was deeply interested in urban planning and architecture. Looking at these streets, I wonder what he'd have to say to the babus in our municipal offices who have so defaced his city.

Amidst ruins, busy markets and badly kept roads, Ghalib's house—whatever little has been preserved—stands like the spirit of a violated land and its exasperated upheavals.

It is in Ghalib's poetry that I found loss, not as an anomaly, a disruption in the usual order of things, but as the point of life itself. His poetry reassured the reader that there will be little solace and zero redress; we will lose everything we love in the end. The only guarantee that comes with life is that it ends. Before it ends, everything you have loved and lost will scorch you blind. Knowing this, Ghalib invites us to not think of grief as a wound, to not carry it as a burden, but to stew in it, like raw mangoes left in brine. To be changed by the process, and to carry the profound sadness that comes with loss lightly. In his lifetime, grief did not diminish him. It expanded his capacity to hold infinite beauty.

I stood in front of Ghalib's house, dripping sweat and trying to avoid traffic in the narrow lanes that were full of good-natured noises and hawkers trying to sell freshly made chai and samosas. If you close your eyes and inhale the masala-laden fragrance from the woks, you could be back in Mughal Dilli. It is said that some of these recipes have remained unchanged through centuries. The fragrance of samosas sputtering in oil touch some intimate fibre of memories that are tied to this city. Like the smell from a good, street-corner hot dog stand in New York or the vinaigrette from the fish and chips sold at Borough Market in London.

The street was an explosion of life, and captured a quintessential aspect of Delhi: an appetite for noise. There were stores on either side, clothes hanging, motorbikes honking, dogs barking, children playing cricket, noises coming from everywhere. Families lived in houses so old they'd be considered worth preserving by any other city administration—not Delhi though. Every successful city is also a cult made up of people who believe in a certain vision of it and are willing to be inconvenienced to achieve it. They will throw garbage in the litter boxes, care for its historical monuments and trees and gardens. Cities without this cultish devotion disintegrate and wither in front of our eyes, like parts of Delhi are withering.

The 'Ghalib walk' cohort walked more slowly, getting in the way of the locals as tourists tend to. Most of us were from 'New' Delhi, and trying to understand what this city might have been like before she got old, bitter and tough as nails. We walked through the lanes Ghalib would have walked, nudging each other, pointing at vintage wooden doors, taking photos of the beautiful architecture from another era. When I imagine this period, the amaltas trees are in full bloom.

For Ghalib, the time he was born in was the greatest curse. The storming of Delhi was an orgy of violence that authors are still writing books about. For the British, though, it was merely a mercantile event—a corporate takeover in which the EIC came to control the Mughal seat of power.

The EIC (1600–1874) was the largest and most successful private enterprise ever created. It is perhaps the primary model for today's conglomerates, like Google, Amazon and Tesla—supra-states—that rule over us. Of course, unlike today's commercial giants, the EIC was allowed to impose its own taxes and raise its own army. All miseries flowed from this foundational one. Though it did not hold sovereignty in the colonies, the EIC was permitted to exercise sovereignty in the name of the British Crown and government. The distinction between the Crown and the Company became further blurred as the EIC became more powerful.

As Britain feathered its nests, some seventeen million Indians died of hunger in the years 1891 to 1900. In 1943, the Bengal famine killed another four million people. By the time it attained Independence, India had been picked clean to the bone. To enable this plunder, the British built India's vast railway network, much as thieves have getaway cars to move the loot quickly.

The Company was impossible to regulate because many members of the British Parliament were either in the EIC employ or were shareholders—23 per cent in the 1770s by one estimate. It was a violent and criminal enterprise from the start, when it was founded in 1600 by a royal charter and was established as a joint-stock trading company.

The Crown then gave it a trading monopoly to exploit opportunities east of the Cape of Good Hope. Crucially, to conduct this trade, the EIC was permitted to 'wage war'. The EIC paid for its own private armies with three army quarters in Bengal, Madras and Bombay, and set up a transnational paramilitary that would make today's oligarchs blush. These armies were run so efficiently that every stakeholder all the way back to London got a piece of the India pie. The already decaying Mughal empire was brought to its knees by the taxes and duties imposed to further enrich the EIC's shareholders and maintain its armed forces.

It was inevitable that its own army would be the Company's downfall.

For Indians, there were many reasons to resent the British, but what eventually sparked off the rebellion of 1857 was religion—a united stand by Hindu and Muslim soldiers against the EIC's efforts to evangelise. The arrival of missionaries had already fuelled rumours about the British wanting to convert Hindus and Muslims to Christianity. Matters came to a head following the introduction of a new gunpowder cartridge for the Pattern 1853 Enfield Rifle. To load the rifle, soldiers had to bite the top off, pour the gunpowder in the barrel and ram it down. Even though the rifle was issued only to the

Europeans, rumours quickly spread that the cartridges for the new rifle were greased with pig and cow fat, making it offensive to both Muslims and Hindus, and adding weight to existing concerns about forced conversion to Christianity.

The mutiny—the largest and bloodiest anti-colonial revolt against any European empire in the nineteenth century—began at Meerut on 10 May 1857. Eighty-five members of the 3rd Bengal Light Cavalry, the Bengal Army of the EIC, who had been jailed for refusing to use cartridges were broken out of prison by their comrades. The mutineers ransacked the nearby military station and killed any Europeans they could find. The following morning, rage-filled and without a strategy, they rode down to Delhi, which was a little over seventy kilometres away.

It is at this point that the mutiny turned into an 'uprising'. For a brief moment, there was a real chance for the revolt to sweep away British control.

On 12 May, a hundred thousand sepoys arrived at Red Fort and called on the Mughal emperor Zafar to lead them. The eighty-two-year-old poet-emperor had already been informed by the EIC that the title would die with him. In 1803, the Company had decided it would benefit them to retain Zafar as a puppet rather than abruptly terminating the Mughal dynasty. They kept the last 'Great Mogul' as a pensioner, in exchange deriving prestige and legitimacy from their hostage. By 1835, the EIC announced that the emperor would be addressed merely as a 'King of Delhi'. Before the year ended, his image was taken off the coinage, with the new rupee bearing the image of the British monarch instead.

Without troops or treasury, Bahadur Shah Zafar gave the mutineers the only thing he could: legitimacy. But he was the wrong man for the moment, and that was the fatal flaw of the mutiny: it had no leader. Zafar held his first formal audience in several years, supporting the rebellion and nominating his eldest surviving son, Mirza Mughal, as commander-in-chief of his forces. Unfortunately, Mirza Mughal had little military experience and was treated with little respect by the sepoys.

No story about Delhi is complete without rage turned inwards.

The rebel army addressed its leadership vacuum by raising princes with no military experience to the status of colonels and generals. The mutineers as well as their leaders would bicker, squabble, grasp for power through the siege of Delhi. The sepoys never agreed on an overall commander, with each regiment refusing to accept orders from any but their own officers. They were without a leader, without weapons and without strategy. The British fought back slowly, strategically, and laid siege to Delhi for four months.

By August, many unpaid sepoys had gone back to the villages. Delhi, which had no role in starting this mutiny, would suffer untold miseries because of it. The city was pushed to famine and disease with no food coming in. By September, elephants from Ferozepur came in, bringing with them the big guns. Cannons were lined up in front of Kashmiri Gate. After four days of heavy artillery firing, on 11 September, the gate was breached. The sepoys fought to their death. By the end of the day, despite all that cannon power, the British had managed to make their way about a hundred yards past the gate, no further. For five days, that battle line held.

On the fifth day, the ill-fated city fell because of a solar eclipse. Hindu soldiers, believing it to be bad luck, stayed indoors during the eclipse. The next morning, when the British woke, they found the trenches deserted. They stepped forward gingerly, thinking it to be a trap. It wasn't. Delhi was declared captured on 21 September 1857. The next morning broke with the roar of royal salute from British guns stationed on the walls of Salimgarh Fort. A British flag waving in the wind said everything there was to say. The city had fallen, and the king was a prisoner in his own palace. It would be another ninety years before Indians could take Delhi back from the British.

The next day, Bahadur Shah's sons and grandson were shot, and the city was declared as captured. Then began a mass slaughter, a fever dream of violence that became known as the 'Devil's Wind'.

For Ghalib, it was a cataclysmic destruction of everything he held dear, his family, his city, his writing. Prominent Muslims were rounded up, Ghalib included, interrogated and tortured. He saw the disappearance of bazaars, he saw Dilli's old havelis razed to the ground. The exquisite court, Diwan-e-Khas, was being used by the troops. The city, now a military camp for the British, had run out of water. Thousands, entire villages, were executed without trial to ensure that there would be no more rebellions. Fearing defilement by the soldiers, many women took their own lives. In some cases, male members killed their female relatives, believing such a death to be better than one that would come after rape. Every male above the age of sixteen was bayoneted. The mutineers were tied to cannon barrels and blown apart. These cannons were fired using only gunpowder cartridge, no cannonball. This led to the dismemberment of the person tied to the muzzle of the cannon. Indians were told to lick up the blood spilt. There was widespread looting of Indian property. In fact, the Hindi word 'loot' got added to the Charles James's *Military Dictionary* in 1802.

In *The Siege of Delhi*, Amarpal Singh writes,

> In the main thoroughfare of the city, Chandni Chowk, a new wooden structure was added in the days after the fall of the city. This was a gallows opposite the *kotwali* where rebels would be hanged in their hundreds over the coming days. A line of rebels was typically led up to the gallows daily, with each man being escorted forward and hanged while those next in line watched before stepping up themselves. A shop was situated near the gallows, and the enterprising owner, sensing an opportunity, began renting out chairs to European spectators. There they could sit and smoke cigars while watching the queue of people snaking forward to meet their maker.

The hangings would continue well into the next year.

Chandni Chowk is now a wholesale market; few of us remember the orgiastic violence that resides in its cellular memory. There were no museums built or memorials at the site of the gallows. I know the place because the historian leading our walk pointed it out. The only images left of Shahjahanabad—what Delhi was then known as—resides in jaded memories of historians and a few books gathering dust on their shelves.

Following the mass slaughter, for a while Delhi lay prostrate, at the mercy of the looters, and the people of Delhi, inconsolable, driven mad with loss. Historian William Dalrymple writes, 'In one neighbourhood alone, Kucha Chelan, 1,400 unarmed citizens were cut down. Delhi, a sophisticated city of half a million souls, was left an empty ruin.' Bodies lay swollen in every stage of decomposition such that horses would slide on body fluids. Ghalib would write, *Their [the British] anger at the citizens of Delhi was so great that, after capturing the city, one would think they would leave not even a dog or a cat alive.*

An account left by Fred Majesty, an army captain, reveals the frenzy of looting inside the Red Fort. 'A motley crowd of troops and followers ransacked every hole and corner, turning everything topsy-turvy in search of the loot. As the men got more and more scattered, the bullets flew more and more avidly.' European civilians joined in the plundering as well. Small items, like the king's cushions in his private pavilions, were seized as trophies.

Captain Majesty took a royal cushion as a memento for his wife. Once the city was stripped of its wealth, British soldiers made more money by demanding ransom to return the ransacked houses to their original owners. If the siege of Delhi lasted four months, the sacking of the city lasted much longer. Plenty of this loot would end up in the museums of London.

As Zafar looked on, his wife Zeenat Mahal handed the crown jewels to Charles Saunders, commissioner of Delhi. Zafar was tried for treason and sentenced to exile in Rangoon (now Yangon, Myanmar). He died there in 1862, bringing the Mughal dynasty to an end. In 1877, Queen Victoria was crowned Empress of India in his place. She'd never set foot in India.

The only solace in the siege of Delhi was that it also ended the rule of the EIC, and the British government decided to run India as a colony. Even though it swept away the Mughal rulers that stood in its path, relentlessly siphoned off resources and made its shareholders eye wateringly rich, the Company could not hide the horror of what had happened in Delhi. As news of its excesses in India reached London, the British Parliament wanted more control over the Company, especially after having recently lost its American colonies. The British Crown took full possession of the EIC's territories in India with the Government of India Act of 2 August 1858. Company armies were absorbed into the British Army, and the EIC navy was disbanded. The most aggressive and utterly ruthless private company ever created was effectively nationalised.

For Ghalib, the Delhi he knew and loved died with the rest of its residents. He would write in *Dastanbuy*, 'five armies, one after the other, invaded the city. First was the army of rebels which robbed the citizens of their reputations; second was the army of *khakhis* (British) who plundered life, property, home, honour, sky, earth and every remnant of life; third was the army of famine at the hands of which thousands perished, even those who were fed were struck down by the fourth army of cholera; the fifth was the army of fever which sapped the endurance and the strength of the people.'

Through this period, Ghalib stayed in Delhi, wading through 'an ocean of blood'. Days after the British occupied Delhi, the army looted Ghalib's wife's jewellery, briefly placed him under arrest and his brother, Mirza Yusuf, died. With no shroud to cover the body, no water to bathe it and no grave-diggers, Ghalib wrote about neighbours helping him with the funeral. He was arrested, accused of high treason and his pension—one he had spent his entire life fighting for—was stopped.

By now, death had almost gained the status of a character in Ghalib's poetry. It is what elevates Ghalib's work above that of his contemporaries: he could capture the difference between grief as mourning rituals—white flowers, funerals and memorial services—and grief as it actually is after the rituals are over: a gaping chasm, unending, vast and silent, made worse by the meaninglessness of it all.

Dastanbuy distils the essence of this meaninglessness in its description of living in a city that was plundered, pillaged and had run out of water, but still somehow housed people who were looking for bread and safety and love. Ghalib's diaries in those days taught me that grief was like water. It could drown you if you don't understand how it works. You can be waterboarded, drown for a bit, come up for air, carry on with your day until suddenly you are waterboarded again. He described Delhi as a garden without a gardener, full of fruitless trees.

He ends his fifteen-month-long diary by noting that none of what he recorded was 'necessary', but he had written it down so that an account reaches people that Delhi was no longer a city where houses were 'lit at night and during the day their chimneys gave forth no smoke. And Ghalib, who had thousands of friends in every house, now in his loneliness, has none to talk with except his pen and no companion except his shadow.'

On 15 February 1869, Ghalib died, leaving Delhi to mourn its most revered poet. He was buried the same afternoon in central Delhi's Nizamuddin Basti in the family graveyard, with all his children. His wife died on the same date, a year later, never having known a day of happiness.

حویلی مرزا غالب
اس حویلی میں ۱۸۶۰ سے ۱۸۶۹ تک
مرزا غالب نے اپنی زندگی کا آخری وقت گزارا
हवेली मिर्ज़ा ग़ालिब
इस हवेली में वर्ष १८६० से १८६९ तक
मिर्ज़ा ग़ालिब ने अपने जीवन का
अन्तिम समय व्यतीत किया।
HAVELI MIRZA GHALIB
MIRZA GHALIB HAD SPENT THE
LAST PHASE OF HIS LIFE IN
THIS HAVELI FROM 1860 TO 1869

There comes a day when you realise the grief is never going away. There were times when my grief seemed to be another being entirely, a parasite dwelling on me, its claws anchored deep in my flesh, swelling and dwindling of its own will. I had not yet come to see how grief can store itself away in the hollows of one's bones.

While I was catatonic with pain, my apartment had turned into a museum of abstract relationships. It had Ali's photos, a skipping rope, that aquamarine cotton sari from my grandmother, her coffee filter, his laptop bag—odd things that stand for what a person used to be. Every object, no matter how trivial, spoke of a life interrupted. Once upon a time it belonged to someone. Not just anyone. Two people I loved dearly. Now they were dead and I had to decide what to do with their things. It felt right to keep them, find use for them. But what use can you find for things when you can barely find use for your own body and mind? Everything felt contaminated, even the house itself felt claustrophobic, like museums do when you spent too much time in them. I didn't want things, and I did not know how to get rid of them.

There's a dream I remember from those years. Paati was there. Ali was there. Some of my close friends, their faces indistinct, just a large dining table filled with food and every seat occupied by people who were smiling, talking, having fun. They—Ali and Paati—are together, sitting next to each other, talking about something. He did not know Tamil and she did not know Hindi, but I took this dream to mean they must've met each other in the afterlife. I imagine them to have liked each other. In the dream, I'm watching them and thinking about how simple and easy happiness can be. This insatiable feeling of wanting something beyond my grasp has never left me.

In reality, I was living my own version of Groundhog Day. I braved the gridlocked, deafeningly loud city to get to work, filed a fruitless 300-word copy and returned home to a deafening silence. I was grief-walking through life. I stopped taking the Ring Road. I stopped going to the restaurants we went to or neighbourhoods we liked. My favourite part of the day was when I'd come back to my apartment and shut the door behind me, not wanting to meet a single person on the other side of that door. I did not like being alone. But I disliked being around people more than I disliked my own company. In a manner of speaking, I now truly belonged to Delhi—the city teaches you to not care about pleasing anyone.

I didn't stop hurting, but I did get better at hiding it. Better at pretending to move on even if I couldn't actually move on. If anyone looked closely—only everyone who would had done so had already died—they'd have seen a paralysed, numb pit of nothingness. This is how things would be for the next decade. Grief also taught me English. Apparently, 'to grieve' is a transitive verb as well as an intransitive one.

Not knowing where to take myself, I'd end up at Ali's grave. Often. His siblings would joke about getting a restraining order against me the few occasions we met for dinner. We would sit with a glass of drink and bowls of food between us, exchanging updates from paths that collided inside a trauma centre. We would never talk about the reason we were there. Instead, his family would tell me about their travels or about people we had in common. I would tell them about the latest story I was reporting. We spoke about elections, books and recipes. It was the stopgap, makeshift language of grief among people who don't really know each other. We would joke about death and death certificates and insurance claim logistics, and about him. The loss was never going to make sense, and so it became funny.

Sometimes, on good mornings, I was able to live again. Play a song or listen to a podcast before that voice in my head reminds me of my dead. I was still struggling to read. I sit staring at the same lines without anything registering. I read that, with time, people are grateful for the grief that cracked their heart in two. That it meant that they loved fully and lived deeply in this unfair, messy life. They say people find beauty within it. How though? After spending nearly a decade trying to make sense of that weekend, this is what I know—that it is entirely possible for pain to be meaningless. There is no point making a mystery out of it. Grief is only grief.

Knowing that doesn't make it easier to come to terms with the meaninglessness of this experience. It has been eleven years, and not a day has gone by where I don't relive some part of that horrible weekend. It is a constant loop in the back of my head, but it no longer causes me to break down. It goes on with other things, like grocery orders or deadlines. There are all sorts of ways to die, of disease, of enmity, of old age or of bad luck. But dying on the streets purely because people are too bored to wear seat belts, drive slower and give way to pedestrians had always felt the most meaningless to me. But now I know I was wrong. In India, we die in meaningless ways everywhere. In Mumbai and at the Maha Kumbh, people die in stampedes. In Kolkata, we can be raped inside government hospitals, and in Chennai, we could die as our homes flood. In Delhi, we die under vehicles. None of India's cities are built with safety in mind. We are like those ancient societies that believe in ritual human sacrifice to pacify the gods.

When I see barricades or checkpoints on Delhi roads, I marvel at the pointlessness of it. This is a city with roads well paved and made for speed, cars driven by the rich who like them to be new and fast, and there is a devastating mismatch between those drive and those who die—the pedestrians, mostly poor. To me, the checkpoints are a little like eating vegetables twice a year while being on an exclusive diet of ice cream for the rest of the year.

I would spend years chasing my need for this suffering to have meaning, to make sense of the years that followed, the weeks, months and years that shredded every idea I had about life and death. I felt the pressure to move on, to live a little. My friends and colleagues were simply bored with me being grief-struck. But the really serious pressure came from Paati and Ali, who I knew would want me to honour their memory by living again. And living well.

Over the years, I have forgotten Ali's face. I have now known the grave for way longer than I ever knew him. I have no idea how to find meaning in what happened and it matters little. What I remember is that he was a lawyer who wanted to help others, a friend who had a generous heart and a family man in an old-fashioned way, a man who found purpose in caring for the people he loved. I want to believe he was—we were—happy before his death. If I had spoken at his memorial service, this is what I would have told his family: he died a happy man. I have since learnt that to die happy, young and make a beautiful corpse is a good way to go.

Every year, as August approached, I'd live through the same nightmare again. Everything I pretended to have healed from would come back to me. I poked at wounds and was always surprised at how they had barely scabbed. It took me years to come to a point where I simply could not live in Delhi anymore.

My immersion in Ghalib's life and times had made me realise that Delhi has always been an angry city—it was forged out of rage, invasion after invasion, and it is no wonder that the people in this city felt comfortable displaying primal anger in the most public manner. Over centuries, grief and rage have remade and shaped this city in equal measure. Even the country's mythology is rooted in anger—in the belief that our discontent can fuel revolutions that can bring down empires.

The city as well as my rage-filled grief had become a familiar prison, and I knew every inch of its walls. I wanted to live somewhere where the raison d'être of my existence was not tending to a grave. Then, one day, I'm not sure when exactly, I took a step—I quit my job, sold my car and gave away furniture. It felt better than sitting and staring at my wounds. I went through the house and stripped photos from every room, emptied out the museum. I'd been looking forward to this almost as much as I had been to leaving Delhi forever. I told myself that it was simply a logistical nightmare of moving houses and adopting a minimalist lifestyle. But if somebody had asked me why it was necessary to time the move in August, tear up documents, give away clothes, empty the kitchen and donate the books, if somebody had pointed out the resemblance to a ritual purge of the life that had been lived in those walls, I would have had to confess to it all. I would have to confess that I was relishing hollowing out the apartment in which, week after week, year after year, I had lived hollowed out by grief.

I planned the end of my relationship with Delhi meticulously. In the years since that weekend, Delhi's winter reliably brought with it apocalyptic air. People got angry, journalists wrote about rising respiratory problems and politicians blamed each other—then we did it all over again the next year. A public health emergency like this would have sparked mass protests in most democracies. But the anger in Delhi is directed only at the powerless. Never to hold power to account.

A week before the fourth anniversary of that wretched weekend, I left this city where people steal the phones of accident victims instead of taking them to the hospital across the road. I changed my number, and for the next seven years, lived out of a suitcase. My first flight was to Srinagar, Kashmir. From there I went to Singapore, where I ate well and ran a lot, then to Guadalajara to report on bovine tuberculosis. Then I went to Montreal, to the beautiful campus of McGill University, and to San Francisco, one of my favourite places in the world. The next year I was in Bangladesh, slumming it out on a freelancer's budget, reporting on the Rohingya genocide. The year after, I lived in a friend's apartment in Mumbai, where I was researching a book. After that, I rented a studio apartment in Goa, furnished entirely with things taken out of storage by the landlord. It was at the mouth of a jungle, and I had to climb up a hill to get a phone network. No one could reach me. I loved it all—the new cities, a fresh perspective, anonymity. By this time, I had changed my phone number and location so many times, I had shaken off all the people from my old life.

In these cities, no one knew me. No one had died on the streets or been buried in the graveyard that I had to cross every day on my way to work. From Goa, I went to Boston. By the time I returned to India, it had been ten years since that horrible weekend in August. I realised I had run far enough. I no longer saw endings as alterable or unalterable. I saw that they were merely meaningless. I had no energy any longer to hate Delhi, to carry that anger in my heart.

It took years of running full throttle from the smell of congealed blood to get here. At some point, I learnt to enjoy my solitude. On the rare occasion I heard myself laugh, it would hurt the way unused muscles hurt. The crushing loneliness of waking up and reliving the deaths was past. As was the white noise of traffic and hospital that could drown me. I could finally hear myself think. And all I wanted now was to be grounded. To literally put down roots, so I started with some mint, chillies and basil. It was the simplest of pleasures—to get my hands dirty, push seeds into the ground and watch them grow. I loved how quickly things grow if you let them, and take over all else around it. I loved the lack of interest plants have in humanity, the quiet cheerfulness of saplings. The peace that came with it was new. Soon there was garlic and passion fruit and mango saplings. Green tips from shoots pushing out all over, at will. Some I planted. Others, like tomatoes and amaranth, simply grew in the compost. Every one of them was a small marvel, a lesson in resilience.

I would call it healing, but to be honest, I had just become used to life being a continual process of loss. Then came the pandemic, a period that will be remembered as one more wave of mass death and all-consuming grief in Delhi's history. The first wave arrived in 2020, killing, by conservative estimates, 1.5 million people. It was a mere raindrop in comparison to the storm that was gathering. The second wave burned through Delhi in the summer of 2021, and its people died in every conceivable way—of hunger, on the streets, in prisons, from suicide, trapped in their car, from oxygen shortage, from non-COVID disease as hospitals were turning patients away, and lastly, of COVID-19. The city was once again bursting with death. News reports and social media posts from the darkest of those days are awash with macabre accounts of desperate people screaming out for scarce oxygen cylinders, hospital beds, ventilators and ambulances—and then for scarce coffins, shrouds and wood for funeral pyres. My activist friends working on the ground went from helping patients find beds to looking for oxygen cylinders to simply helping by moving the dead away from the dying. Delhi turned into a disaster zone, and for days, ashes rained on terraces close to crematoriums.

Nobody prepares you for loss at this scale. Everyone who lived through those times lost friends, colleagues, neighbours, relatives. The only mercy was that the virus killed quickly. From April through July of 2021, once again, Delhi lay prostrate, at the mercy of the plague. While every city had its share of horrors, Delhi saw people die like the wretches of fourteenth-century Sicily facing wave after wave of Black Death—bodies rotting by the roadside in the summer heat as crematoriums ran out of space.

In those dark days, the grace shown by the people of Delhi towards each other was the only thing that kept it going. Watching the people of this city I always accused of indifference turn up for each other, I was surprised by how Delhi could still tug at my heart. Between government mismanagement and a virulent virus, the odds were simply stacked against the people. But watching the city try, and fail, it felt worthy of some sort of an ovation.

The frustrating thing about Delhi is that so much of it is horrible. For every child that is cared for and nurtured, there is one loose on the street, malnourished, begging at the nearest traffic signal. For every girl who's safe, loved and respected, there are ten beaten, broken, humiliated. For every Good Samaritan, there are a hundred mean-spirited people around us. But the few who are good, they make this city tick. The people who let pedestrians pass, leave water out in the summer for stray animals, recycle wet waste to not add more to landfill and smile at strangers with kindness and thank the barista for making the coffee. Little acts that come out of large, spacious hearts. They save our world, not with big, spectacular, heroic acts but by ordinary acts of kindness. In quiet ways they are making it better just by being in it. They show how beautiful this city could be. The few good ones, the Good Samaritans are not only a marvel in a city like this but also its saving grace.

Amidst all the loss, I decided it was worth the effort to gather up the fragments and attempt the Sisyphean task of putting my life in order. Or as much order as one could have while being constantly on the move. When I travelled, the herbs would die. I'd buy more seeds, start over. The attempt at the kitchen garden, in my mind, had the frail, audacious permanence of a bird's nest on the edge of a branch. It may be held together by twigs and wisps of leaves, but it keeps the lives entrusted to it safe night after night for years. And so it was—things were unstable, but life was marching forward, dragging me along. I had stopped fantasising about the life I could not live. I liked waking up without nightmares, having a small kitchen that would meet my grandmother's approval. A deep couch in which I could read a book comfortably. Coffee always brewing. I could be happy with this kind of joy—

small, simple, temporary—that you are truly grateful for once you have accepted death.

I don't think I resent Delhi anymore. In fact, over the years, my dirty secret was that I kept trying to return 'home'—for my arthritic heart, sometimes it meant old restaurants in my old neighbourhoods, sometimes it was old friends or books about the city—things which would have offered comfort to the person I used to be a lifetime ago.

The people of this city are strange creatures. They'll come to blows over a delayed flight, slow traffic and tepid coffee. But when it comes to the real deal—life-or-death questions like poisoned air, begging children and raped women—we barely flinch. I see now that we rage at the small stuff because of its smallness, its quantifiable, solvable smallness. The big stuff, if we said a word about it, it would unspool more words and the entire edifice of rage and deceit would lie exposed to our eyes.

Perhaps Ghalib did not love Delhi because she was great. She was great because he and men like him loved her. Today, Delhi is unloved more than she has ever been. The city that rose from its ashes every time it was ruined is perhaps ready for one last ruining. That's probably what we are witnessing every day as we drive past landfills in Ghazipur, breathe in the poisonous air and rush, rush,

rush. Everyone who lives in Delhi is playing Jenga, the board game where each party gets a turn to make the situation worse, cumulatively leading to a total collapse. When that comes, when the air is entirely poisoned, the roads are terrifying and the water is toxic, we place the blame on the person with least power—the farmer in Punjab or the pedestrian trying to navigate a road without footpaths or the family living in the urban slum who wash their clothes in the Yamuna. Meanwhile, the city dies, of smog or traffic or riots or all of these. What causes the end will simply be a matter of record.

Perhaps it is in Delhi's nature to be marvellously generous while bleeding out. Perhaps that's always been her fate—to rot and to rise. To die and glow at the same time. To be Ouroboros. All one can hope is that it wouldn't have been in vain. The sweeping away of thousands of lives ought to hold lessons. For other people in other cities.

I don't go to Delhi often, but I was there in May 2024 to vote. As my flight began its descent, I thought of the rage-induced promise I had made to never set foot in this city again. But here I was, to prove to myself that I could walk along these streets, no longer mine, travel through it like a tourist and not have it provoke bitterness, grief, rage or nostalgia in me.

Ghalib's world was still intact, especially in his poetry, which contained his capacity to experience oceanic grief without losing the ability to love. He teaches us that things don't end in poetry. They end in blood, and we turn it into poetry.

Truth is, I will grieve for them forever. I will never be whole again, but I will also not be the same either, which is its own mercy. In the last decade, I learnt about the mechanics of grieving, and the endless different ways to grieve. There is wearing black and performing the rituals associated with death. That's one way. There is also going quiet and farther from everyone else, or not answering phone calls and changing phone numbers and moving to cities where you're likely to be alone. There is daytime mourning behind sunglasses, and there is night-time mourning when you stare at the ceiling. There is car mourning and Delhi mourning and Boston mourning, and when you do it long enough, all of it seeps into your bone marrow and makes you wail and wail and wail, but no tears come. But it is also possible to listen to music and to dance while mourning. It is possible to smile at strangers, make new friends and read good books too. It is possible to carry the dead without being weighed down by them.

After having voted, I went back to the neighbourhood where Ghalib lived in those terrible days of 1857. Amidst the chaos of the megapolis that is Delhi, the last great poet of the Mughal era lies forgotten, emptied of his poetry. The ancient archway leads to his nineteenth-century courtyard on the left and a travel agency on the right. I believe Delhi hurt him into poetry. Delhi remains hurtful still because poetry does not change anything. It simply survives. And Ghalib's gift survived it all: physical decay, the chaos of the centuries that came after. The recognition he yearned in life is now his. Young people carry tote bags and postcards with Ghalib's face on them. It isn't the face of a man who's masculine or aristocratic or handsome. The image is neither young nor old. He could be middle-aged. He could also be a thousand years old. Timeless like trees or animals that bear scars from wounds they simply can't speak of.

I think I know what he'd say, if he knew about everything that followed—Indian Independence, the end of the British empire, the joys, the grief, the neglect and the tote bags and all the other things lost along the way.

Dard minnat-kash-e-davā na huā
Maiñ na achchhā huā burā na huā
My pain does not seek favours from opium
I don't mind the fact that I never recovered

In the twenty minutes I was at Ghalib's home, no one stopped by. Someone had left flowers under his photo not too long ago. I went from his residence to his grave in Nizamuddin. From there, I walked over to Ali's grave not too far away, left white lilies, then left for the airport.

ACKNOWLEDGEMENTS

The stories in these pages were conceived as an essay for *Granta* magazine, but they insisted on becoming a book. Writing it has been an extraordinary journey, and I am deeply grateful to all the remarkable people who helped bring it to life.

First, my heartfelt thanks to the Nieman Foundation, Class of '21—my shelter in the storm. To Steve Almond, for being there from the very beginning. To Ann Marie Lipinski, for everything.

To Roman Gautam, my first reader, always on point.

A special thank you to Karthika V.K., Ajitha G.S., Rukun Kaul and the brilliant team at Westland, who gave my words a home. I owe a great deal of thanks to Ajitha, in particular, for her careful and thoughtful guidance throughout the production process.

To Chitra Maudgil, a gifted designer and fellow traveller—your vision means more than words can express. To Dylan Smeder, my hiding place.

To Nandini Sharma, Pratiksha Rao, Siddharth Singh, Mushtari Sayed and Mandakini Gahlot—for simply being there.

Muneeza Naqvi.

Finally, to the readers—it is all for you, always.

Thank you.